DATE DUE

MY 20 '89	AG 9 '90	AUG 6 92	
JE 6 '89	AG 16 '90	MAR 19 '90	N 03 17
JE 21 '8	AG 30 '90	JUL 1 5	
JY 5 '89	NO 17 '90	OCT 21 94	
JY 26 '89	DE 1 2 '90	NOV 1 0 94	
AG 11 '89	FE 5 '91	MAR 1 7 '97	
AG 22 '89	MR 9 '91	JY 20 00	
OC 5 '8	MR 25 '91	MY 10 03	
OC 25 '89	JY 15 '91	SE 20 04	
MR 20 '90	AG 9 '91	SE 02 04	
JY 3 '90	AG 13 '91	SE 18 '04	
JY 19 '90	MR 4 '92		

$10.60

E
KOR
Korman, Justine
Who framed Roger Rabbit:
a different toon

A Different Toon

Based on the motion picture from
Walt Disney Pictures and Steven Spielberg

Executive Producers

STEVEN SPIELBERG   KATHLEEN KENNEDY   FRANK MARSHALL

Produced by
ROBERT WATTS
Screenplay by
JEFFREY PRICE & PETER SEAMAN
Directed by
ROBERT ZEMECKIS
Storybook adapted by
JUSTINE KORMAN
Illustrated by
AL WHITE STUDIOS

A GOLDEN BOOK • NEW YORK
Western Publishing Company, Inc., Racine, Wisconsin 53404

There was once a place called Toontown, where the stars of the animated cartoons lived ...and anything could happen.

Roger Rabbit was a Toon falsely accused of a crime. He was running from a weasel Toon Patrol with the help of a detective named Eddie Valiant.

Roger and Eddie hid from the weasels in a
movie theater. Roger forgot all his troubles and
laughed at the cartoons on the screen.

But Eddie Valiant never even cracked a smile.

Breathless from laughing, Roger managed to ask, "Why aren't you laughing, Eddie? Don't you like cartoons?"

Valiant shook his head. "I don't like cartoons and the useless Toons who make them. And I haven't laughed at anything in years."

Roger was stunned and hurt.

"I'm sorry you feel that way, Eddie," Roger said. "Laughter can sometimes be the best solution to a problem."

Eddie didn't answer. Just then, one of the cartoons came to an end and Roger and his co-star, Baby Herman, appeared on the screen.

"That gives me an idea," Eddie announced. "I think I'm going to visit the Maroon Cartoon Studio to question R. K. Maroon. I have a feeling he might be mixed up in all this somehow."

Roger gulped. "R.K. is a pretty tough customer," he told the detective.

Eddie shrugged. "If I don't come back—"

"Then neither will I," Roger interrupted, hardly believing his long ears. "I'm going with you. After all, I'm the one who got you into this."

The pair left the theater and headed for the Maroon Studios.

In the hall outside R.K.'s office Valiant paused and told his companion, "You don't have to stay if you're scared."

Roger's rabbit feet almost started to run. His buck teeth chattered with fear. But he stood his ground and tried not to let his voice shake when he replied, "I'm right behind you, Eddie."

Unfortunately, someone was right behind
Roger, too. And as soon as Eddie turned his
back, that someone leapt out of the shadows and
bonked Roger over the head.

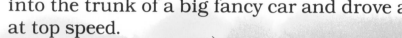

Eddie heard Roger fall and turned just in time to see the rabbit being dragged out the door. He chased Roger's attacker, who threw the rabbit into the trunk of a big fancy car and drove away at top speed.

When Eddie caught up to the car at a
stoplight, he was surprised to see Jessica, a
glamorous Toon, behind the wheel. "This case
gets stranger by the minute," he mused. "I
thought Jessica was Roger's best friend!"

Then the light changed, and the big car took
off with Eddie in pursuit.

Jessica parked in the heart of Toontown and ran off on foot. Eddie pulled the rabbit out of her trunk, but Roger was too groggy to help. So Eddie followed Jessica through winding streets and back alleys.

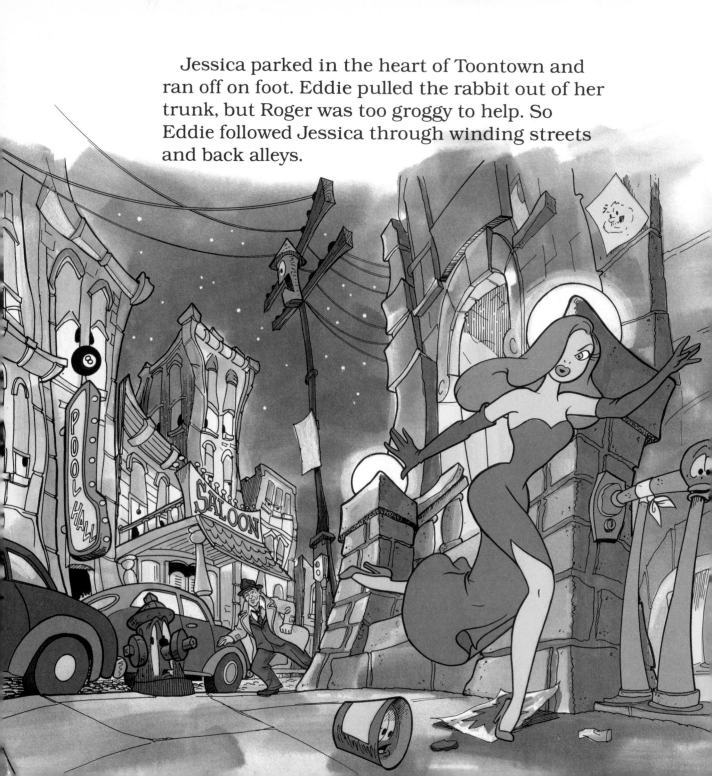

At last he cornered the beautiful Toon.
"Why did you bonk the bunny?" Eddie demanded.
Jessica's eyes filled with tears. "It was the only
way I could think of to get him out of there. The
studio was full of weasels hunting for Roger, because
Judge Doom is determined to get rid of him."

"Don't be ridiculous," Eddie scoffed. "No one can get rid of a Toon." Toons were always getting flattened by steamrollers and dropped off cliffs in their movies, but they never seemed to get too badly hurt.

Jessica explained with a shudder, "Doom's invented this stuff called the Dip that dissolves us into a puddle of ink. And Doom wants to Dip Roger because he's the only one who can stop Doom from taking over Toontown.

"Won't you help us?" Jessica asked with a pleading look in her perfect green eyes.

Valiant shrugged. Why should he care about Toontown? Then he remembered. "A Dipped rabbit can't pay my fee," Eddie observed. "Let's find this Doom and arrest him."

"I've got a feeling that Doom's gang is
somewhere near here," Jessica whispered.
    Suddenly the alley was alive with weasels, and
a horrible laugh boomed from the darkness.
    "You are surrounded," cackled Judge Doom,
his cape fluttering like the wings of a giant bat.

Soon Eddie and Jessica were tied up and
taken to the abandoned Gag Factory.
"Roger will save us," Jessica shouted bravely.
But Doom only laughed his terrible laugh. And
Eddie couldn't help thinking the gloomy judge
was right. No crazy Toontown rabbit...

Just then, Roger burst through the factory door.
"Let them go, Doom!" the rabbit commanded,
surprised at the forceful sound of his own voice.
"Didn't I tell you Roger would save us?" Jessica
cooed with pride.

Eddie looked up at the sound of a weasel's giggle.
"Look out!" he shouted to Roger as a ton of cartoon
bricks was dropped on the poor rabbit from above.
Doom laughed so hard his cape billowed like a
storm cloud. He was laughing so much that he
didn't see Eddie slip out of the ropes that held him.

"Prepare to be Dipped!" Doom hissed to Roger and Jessica. "Shall I start at your feet or your heads?"

But before they could answer, Eddie remembered what Roger had said about laughter. He startled them all by bursting into a crazy song and dance. The words of his song were so funny that the weasels laughed themselves dizzy.

"Stop it, you weasels!" Doom thundered.

But the weasels only laughed harder, which gave Eddie a chance to dance over to a box of itching powder. He threw a whole box at the giggling guards, and soon they were too busy scratching to stop Eddie.

Doom bellowed with rage and lunged for Eddie. But his foot slipped on a plastic banana peel, and Doom fell into the Dip. Soon nothing was left except Doom's cape.

"Doom was a Toon?!" Roger asked in amazement.

"One very evil Toon," Eddie replied thoughtfully. Then he smiled at Roger. "I guess some Toons are good and some Toons are bad. They're just like people."

"Not quite like people," Roger said, bopping himself with a punching bag.

Eddie laughed at the beautiful ring of stars that danced around Roger's head. It felt good to laugh again, Eddie thought, as he, Roger, and Jessica left the factory and walked into the night.